DAY OF THE DEAD

DAY OF THE DEAD

Tony Johnston

Illustrated by Jeanette Winter

Harcourt Brace & Company

San Diego   New York   London

Library of Congress Cataloging-in-Publication Data
Johnston, Tony, 1942–
Day of the Dead/Tony Johnston;
illustrated by Jeanette Winter.
p. cm.
Summary: Describes a Mexican family preparing for
and celebrating the Day of the Dead.
ISBN 0-15-222863-2
[1. All Soul's Day—Mexico—Fiction. 2. Mexico—Fiction.]
I. Winter, Jeanette, ill. II. Title.
PZ7.J6478Day 1997
[E]—dc20 96-2276

F

Printed in Singapore

The illustrations in this book were done in acrylics
on Strathmore Bristol paper.
The display type was set in Serif Gothic Heavy.
The text type was set in Barcelona Medium.
Color separations by Bright Arts, Ltd., Singapore
Printed and bound by Tien Wah Press, Singapore
Production supervision by Stanley Redfern and Pascha Gerlinger
Designed by Jeanette Winter and Kaelin Chappell

For Jeanette Winter.
And in memory of
Josefina Leal.
—T. J.

In memory of
Signe Maria Ragner.
—J. W.

Above a small town in Mexico,
the sun rises
like a great marigold.

A soft sound comes from a warm kitchen.
Slap, slap. Slap, slap.
The children hear it and wake up.

Mamá is making *empanadas*,
little pastries fat with meat.

The children crowd around.
"*¡Una probadita!* A taste!"
"Wait," says *mamá*. "*Espérense.*"
"Till when?"
"Soon."

For weeks the family
has been preparing for this day.
Los tíos, the uncles, have picked fruit.
Bright oranges, red apples, *tejocotes* of gold.

The children have tried to sneak the fruit.
"Wait," say *los tíos*. "*Espérense.*"
"Till when?"
"Soon."

For days *las tías*, the aunts, have been grinding dry *chiles* to powder.

The children have been sniffing the *chile* powder
and sneezing.
"Wait," say *las tías*.
"HA-CHOO!" The children sneeze.

For days *papá* has been visiting the bakery,
bringing back bulging bundles.

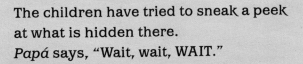

The children have tried to sneak a peek
at what is hidden there.
Papá says, "Wait, wait, WAIT."

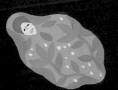
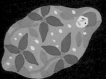

For days *mamá* has baked *pan de muertos*, bread of the dead.

The children have tried to sneak
pan de muertos to eat.
"*¿Ni una miga?*" they ask.
"No," *mamá* says. "Not one crumb."

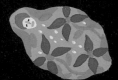
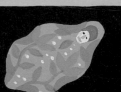

For nights all the family has been making *tamales* for this day.

The children have tried to sneak *tamales* to eat. *"Espérense."*

Today *papá* has cut up long wands of *caña*, sugarcane.

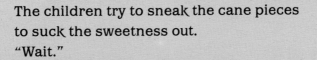

The children try to sneak the cane pieces
to suck the sweetness out.
"Wait."

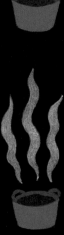
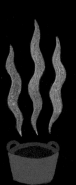
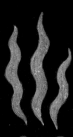

Today *las tías* brew a sauce of *chocolate*
and *chile*—a *mole*.
They put chicken in, stirring, stirring again.

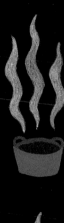

The children try to sneak the *mole*—just a taste.
"*Espérense,*" the stirring aunts say.

The children come from the market
with loads of *zempasúchil,* marigolds.

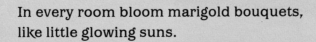

In every room bloom marigold bouquets,
like little glowing suns.

Now night has come.

The family gathers all the things
they have made for this day.
And they go out into the night.

Families from all the houses come carrying all the things they have made.

Carrying marigolds bright as suns.
And candles like stars.

The little procession goes walking
through the street.
Walking over the hill, walking to
the graveyard where their loved ones lie.

They go dropping a path of petals
for the spirits to find their way.

The family comes to the graves of *los abuelos*, the grandparents.

There they place salt and water in small bowls.
And they place all the things they have made.

They sing.

And they dance.

And they remember *los abuelos*.

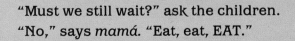

"Must we still wait?" ask the children.
"No," says *mamá*. "Eat, eat, EAT."

Papá unwraps his bundles.
¡Calaveras de azúcar! Sugar skulls!
The children squeal and eat this treat.

Mamá slices *pan de muertos.*
Everyone tastes the sweet bread.
One child bites his and—*¡Ay-ay-ay!*—he finds
the tiny, skinny skeleton *mamá* baked inside!

Now it is late.
The family gathers what is left
of all the things they have brought.
They gather platters, jugs, and jars.

They gather their sleeping children.

Upon the graves they leave the marigolds.

Then they go walking, walking home,
carrying candles like stars.

AUTHOR'S NOTE

The Day of the Dead, *El día de los muertos*,
is one of Mexico's most important holidays.
It actually spans three days, from October 31
to November 2, and is a time to remember
loved ones now gone. Families prepare favorite
foods of the departed and picnic at their
graves. They adorn the graves with marigolds,
the traditional flower of the dead, and strew
paths of petals to lead the spirits to the
offerings, which, along with the delicious food,
usually include salt and water, symbols of
ongoing life. The people dance, sing, and share
memories of their loved ones, welcoming their
spirits, who are thought to return briefly to
take part in the celebration.